Dear
Garbage
Man

Dear Garbage

by Gene Zion

Man

Pictures by Margaret Bloy Graham

A TRUMPET CLUB SPECIAL EDITION

Published by
The Trumpet Club
666 Fifth Avenue
New York, New York 10103

Text copyright © 1957 by Eugene Zion
Pictures copyright © 1957 by Margaret Bloy Graham

The Trademark Dell® is registered in the U.S. Patent and Trademark Office.
ISBN: 0-440-84200-X

Reprinted by arrangement with Harper & Row, Publishers, Inc.
Printed in the United States of America
November 1988

10 9 8 7 6 5 4 3 2

Stan was a new garbage man.
He was happy and excited
this lovely spring morning because
it was his first day on the truck.
In the trash put out the night before
in front of "Emily's Hat Shoppe,"
Stan found a horseshoe made of flowers.
On the ribbon were the words,
"Best Luck to Emily."

Stan liked the name "Emily"
so he didn't throw the horseshoe into
the chewer-upper at the back of the truck.
He tied it on the front.

When people saw the truck, they laughed and said,
"Look, here comes Emily! Isn't she pretty?"
Stan felt very pleased and was glad that he
had kept the flower horseshoe and ribbon.

At the next stop, Stan saw an old bed that had
been put out on the sidewalk to be taken away.
"Someone can use this. Let's save it," he said.
. . . "And let's save that fine bicycle too."

Just as the men were about to break up an old sofa
so that Emily could chew it more easily,
Stan said, "With a little fixing, this would be as
good as new. Let's save it and make someone happy."

Stan threw very little in the chewer-upper.
It wasn't because Emily couldn't hold any more ...
she could chew up any amount of trash very easily.
Stan wanted to save <u>everything</u>!

He saved something at each stop Emily made . . .
a cracked mirror, part of a soda fountain,
a baby carriage and a piece of wooden fence.
Emily got taller and taller.

When the driver looked out,
he decided that Stan had collected enough.
He drove on without making any more stops.

"Whoa, not so fast!" cried Stan. "You're passing all the best stuff!" The driver shrugged his shoulders, stopped and backed up. Stan saved a bridge lamp, a broken bird cage, an old awning and a bass drum.

"What a wonderful play pen!" cried Stan.
"And did you ever see such lovely picture frames?"
The driver could hardly see where he was going
because of the pile on the front.

Emily moved very slowly, swaying from side to side,
as the cars honked behind her.
The whole neighborhood was whistling and cheering.

"All right, folks, help yourselves!" Stan shouted.
"Take what you like!"
There was a loud cheer.

The garbage men shook Stan's hand
and slapped him on the back.
They had never seen <u>anything</u> like this.

Some people took things right through their windows.
Others on the sidewalk gathered around Emily

shouting, "Look at this!" "How wonderful!"
"Just what I need!" "Just what I've always wanted!"

After everyone had helped themselves,
fathers went to work and mothers went back
to the dishes. Boys and girls went off to school,
eager to tell their friends all about Emily.

The pile on the truck was all gone.
The other garbage men told Stan how smart he was
and then they all climbed back on the truck.
The only thing left was Emily's horseshoe.

Emily's last stop was at the river.
Here everything that had been collected and
chewed up in the trucks was loaded onto barges.
The boss garbage man walked over to Emily.
"Where's <u>your</u> load, boys?" he asked.

"We gave it all away," Stan answered happily.
The boss gulped and almost swallowed his cigar.
"You don't say!" he exclaimed.
Then he rubbed his chin and slowly said,
"Well, no one ever did _that_ before."

That night as the city slept, the tugboats chugged
and whistled softly as they pulled the barges
down the river. The trash and ashes they carried
would be used to fill in swampland.
Then parks and playgrounds would be built there.

But Stan didn't hear the tugboats whistling
as they pulled their heavy load. He was
fast asleep, dreaming of all the useful things
he would save and give away the next day.
Stan was the happiest garbage man in the city.

In the morning at the garage, Emily's crew changed into their work clothes. Everyone called Stan "The Sanitation Department's Santa Claus."

The driver started Emily's engine, and a mechanic straightened her flower horseshoe.
The men shouted goodbye, and off they went to work.

When they rounded the corner of the first street
in their district, Stan took one look and gasped.

There on the sidewalk, up and down the street, were
all the things that he had given away the day before.

The truck stopped and Stan got off. He walked slowly
past the old bicycle, the baby carriage, the lamp and
the picture frames. When he got to the bed,
he stopped. There was a note tacked to its side.

It said, "Dear Garbage Man: I'm sorry but the bed was older and more broken than we thought . . . you'd better give it to Emily. Thanks anyway. . . . A Friend."
When Stan finished reading, he seemed ready to cry.

But suddenly, a big smile brightened his face
and he began to drag the bed to the truck.
"Start the chewer-upper, boys!" he shouted.
"All this stuff will fill in <u>lots</u> and <u>lots</u> of swamps!"
The chewer-upper started, and Emily's horseshoe
jiggled up and down. The driver leaned out and yelled,
"Stan, you're a <u>real</u> garbage man now!"